The Trail of 1

H. Bedford-Jones

Alpha Editions

This edition published in 2024

ISBN : 9789357963602

Design and Setting By
Alpha Editions
www.alphaedis.com
Email - info@alphaedis.com

As per information held with us this book is in Public Domain.
This book is a reproduction of an important historical work. Alpha Editions uses the best technology to reproduce historical work in the same manner it was first published to preserve its original nature. Any marks or number seen are left intentionally to preserve its true form.

THE TRAIL OF DEATH

BY H. BEDFORD-JONES

> "Over Abbeville," the second in this remarkable series, includes one of the most unusual and exciting scenes ever described—a fight to the death waged in the narrow cabin of a London-to-Paris passenger plane.

Durant stood at the rail, watching the gleam of the Land's End light twinkle across the night. The *Tyrania* was on the last leg of her voyage; at dawn she would be just off Plymouth, and all those who could change at the last moment would go into the lighter instead of on to Cherbourg, for dirty weather lay ahead of her. Durant had changed, but for other reasons.

A light step, and Durant turned to find the slender figure of Baroness Glincka at his side. Known aboard ship as Mrs. Robinson, her unhappy story was hidden with her name; only Durant knew how her dead husband's cousin, Boris Makoff, held her gripped in tentacles of blackmail, forcing her to aid his little schemes, making her an unwilling but helpless member of his Paris coterie of genteel crooks. It was for her sake that Durant had wormed his way into this organization, getting the confidence of Makoff—waiting!

"You got the message?" she asked in the darkness.

"Yes, and changed. You'll get off at Plymouth too?"

"Yes. Boris is planning something at London, before going on. I'm not sure what; but the victim is that white-haired man who keeps to himself. Larson, the name is. Boris introduced him to me tonight, using my real name. He's a nice old man."

"And a game's on, eh?" Durant knew Larson by sight—a stiff, bronzed man with white hair and mustache, and shrewd, kindly old eyes, traveling alone.

"Something. Boris wants you to come into the smoking-room, and meet Larson. I think he's a Dane who's made a fortune in America and is taking a trip to Denmark—that's my guess. I suppose Boris means to wring his neck in London by your help and mine."

"Pleasant prospect," said Durant.

"What will Lewis say when he learns the truth?"

"He won't learn it. I've arranged—at a little expense. You'll see in the morning."

"Then you're a magician!"

"Borrowed magic—from your beauty."

She laughed a little and was gone into the darkness. Durant stared out at the gleaming light on the horizon, and thought over the past, back to those Paris days when he, a clerk in an American branch bank, poor, half-starved, struggling for life and health, had seen the beautiful Baroness Glincka come in three times a week to the next window.

And now he knew her, was fighting for her—was a crook for her sake! An odd turn of destiny. An almost forgotten relative dead, a legacy of almost forgotten land in Florida, a trip home—wealth! Then he headed back for Paris, to take his ease where he had starved and fought and sweated. So he had thought—but work had come to him.

"That you, Durant?" It was the voice of Lewis, who came quietly out of the darkness, a cigar-tip glowing redly. "First sight of England, eh? I'm leaving you in the morning."

"But I'm going up to London too, instead of on to Cherbourg."

"Good! Shall I see you in London?"

"No. Wiser not—wait for Paris."

"Right. I'll give you my address there. I'm going right on—taking the afternoon plane over tomorrow."

Lewis fumbled for a card-case. He was a smallish man, very alert—a wholesale druggist from the Middle West, now engaged in smuggling a suitcase filled with cocaine into France—a task in which Durant presumably was aiding. True, Durant had saved him from Boris Makoff, had dumped the cocaine into the Atlantic and substituted baking soda for it—and for these services, known and unknown, Lewis was an ally. Once in Paris, he promised to be a most important ally.

"Thanks." Durant took the card thrust at him. "You'll hear from me as soon as I get settled—if not before! I've a rather big game to pull off, and there'll be pickings in it. They'll go to your friends who help me. I'm not in it for money."

He did not say that he was not in it for crooks' money—he had no intention of injuring the feelings of Lewis just yet. The two men separated, and Durant headed for the smoking-room, filled to bursting with the usual last-night crowd.

Makoff had a table and lounge in one corner; with him was the silent, rather offish Larson—impeccably dressed, as usual, and only a little less lonely. Helen—or Baroness Helena Glincka—had rejoined them and was drawing Larson into almost lively conversation. Cards lay waiting on the table.

Durant approached, saw Makoff make a remark, saw the eyes of Larson sweep to him with almost eager interest. He could not understand it, but came up to the table. Makoff rose.

"Ah, Durant! Let me introduce you to Mr. Larson of Toledo—Mr. Durant. What about a rubber, if your packing's done?"

"Glad." Durant bowed to the Baronne, and shook hands with Larson, in whose mild blue eyes rested that same curious, scrutinizing expression. Then and later his manner toward Durant was almost deferential, though as a rule his air was brusque enough. That he was quite captivated by the Baronne, too, was soon evident.

There was no opportunity for private conversation until, a few rubbers ended, Helen departed under pretense of having to pack. Larson also rose, and shook hands with Durant.

"If you're alone," he said, "we might go to London together in the morning."

"I'll be glad," said Durant, finding himself liking the old man. "See you at the pier, eh?"

So they parted. Left alone, Durant met the gaze of Makoff with inquiring eyes.

"Well? What's the game?"

The bold, aggressive regard of the Russian dwelt upon him for an instant, and in those dark depths Durant read startling, baffling things.

"Tell you later," said Makoff calmly, with a gesture at the room. "Get up to London with him, ask him to visit you for a day or so—until Monday, say. The week-end. Tell him your car will meet the train."

"My car? But I haven't any!"

"Your mistake," said Makoff, and smiled. "Your chauffeur, Giles, will meet the train." And this was all he would say.

In the drizzling rain of a dark gray dawn, the *Tyrania* disembarked her passengers into the lighter, while the rattling, banging winches sent aboard the nets of hold luggage. Durant stood in the rain on the upper deck of the lighter, watching.

"I've been looking for you." The Baronne emerged from the cabin, joined him. Her face was pale, anxious, her sky-blue eyes wide and filled with alarm. "I've learned what's up—"

Durant, touching his hat, turned suddenly to the rail. "Look!" he broke in. There was a swift commotion forward—angry cries, orders, a medley of voices. One of the nets had just come down.

"What is it?" she demanded, frowning at the rain-wet scene. Durant laughed.

"That," he said, "is the pet suitcase of our friend Lewis going over the side. It's gone! Here's the sequel." And he opened his hand to show a twenty-pound note. "But you were going to say—"

She came close to him. "I've found out about it," she said rapidly in French. "I think Larson's to be murdered—I'm not sure. He's carrying a large sum—got it from the purser—in cash."

"I'll take care of it," said Durant, and took her hand. He smiled into her eyes. "Out of the rain, now! All's well that ends well. *Au revoir!*"

The last Durant saw of Lewis, the little rascal was involved in heated argument at the Customs shed with sundry porters. Durant laughed and passed on. His own trail was covered; the cocaine and substitute alike were gone; and the past was closed. The future remained.

Closeted in a first-class compartment with Larson, Durant arranged about breakfast, took his companion into the restaurant car, and thawed him out in no time. Returning, they lighted cigars and became more or less confidential. Durant found himself treated with the same curious interest he had noticed the previous evening, but could not penetrate to the reason.

Larson was shyly eloquent regarding the Baronne. A shrewd old man, manufacturer and banker, he was yet in some ways diffident and unsophisticated as a child—and Makoff had obviously found the way, though Durant was slow to realize just where it lay. Comprehension came slowly.

"Perhaps you'll stay the week-end with me?" asked Durant. "I'm not going on to Paris at once, and I'd be very glad. You see, I've been rather alone."

"Like me," said Larson. "Yes, I noticed. Queer we'd run together the last day! Why, about the visit—I don't know, Durant, I don't know. I'd like to mighty well, but I expect I'd make a fool of myself. I'm not acquainted with the way you do things over here."

Durant was puzzled, the more so because he himself was acting in the dark, not knowing what Makoff intended.

"And she was a real baroness, eh?" Larson chewed his cigar. "Well, well! And to think of you—but I suppose you don't imagine that I know who you are? But I do. That's why I'm afraid to accept your invitation. I'd like to, because I like you; anyone can see you're straight as a string, in spite of what they say about nobility. Now, I'm not so sure about that Russian chap—"

"Nobility?" repeated Durant. Larson broke into a laugh.

"Oh, I know about it! That Russian told me. You see, so long as you're Durant to me, it's all right. We get on fine. But when you become Lord Northcote—gosh, man! I'd be proud enough to bust, to think I'd visited you—but think of the breaks I'd make! I wouldn't know whether to call you 'My Lord,' or 'Mister,' or what! And being all alone, with my wife dead, I've no one to steer me around. Not but what it's tempting—"

Durant laughed, largely to conceal his startled amazement, for the old man's loneliness struck him as pathetic. Lord Northcote!

"So I'm a lord, am I?" he said. Larson chuckled.

"Oh, he warned me you'd perhaps be angry—but I'll say nothing about it. You just keep on being Durant, see? If you will, I'll accept the invitation. How about it? I'll have three days in London anyhow. Leaving there Monday."

"Done," said Durant.

He probed carefully, anxious to make no slip, and came upon the amazing truth. Larson, a Continental by birth, had profound respect for nobility; now, old and wealthy, going back to Europe, the idea of mixing with titled gentry was fascinating in the extreme to him—it was his weak spot.

And lurking in the background behind all this, was black murder.

Warn Larson? Impossible. Against his plans and hopes for rescuing Helen Glincka from the blackmail grip of Makoff, Durant would have let a dozen Larsons go to death. Being a party to it was another matter altogether, and here he could act as events gave him clue. He was well assured that Makoff would have made careful plans by wire, for the Russian had a very able criminal organization to back him up; warning Larson, then, might only precipitate the disaster.

Sooner or later, a break must come with Makoff—indeed, Durant meant to attack the man mercilessly, pitilessly, upon reaching Paris. There he would be on familiar ground, and would have friends among the dope-ring, thanks to Lewis; he could fight fire with fire. Until then, he must inform himself as fully as possible about Makoff's crowd, arm himself with every possible weapon, prepare!

"I'll have to play my part, save Larson if possible, keep under cover with Makoff," he decided. And aloud: "My car should meet the train—have you any luggage?"

"Just my two suitcases." Larson pointed at the rack. Then he smiled. "I'm keeping close to them, too! One of 'em has a big roll of currency—more than I could carry, for I have my pockets full besides."

"Eh?" Durant stared, wondering at such recklessness. "You're not serious?"

Larson chuckled. "Think it queer, eh? Well, it is! But in the old country, you know,—and all over Europe for that matter,—American money is badly wanted. Not in gold, because it's not pure, but bills. So I'm bringing back a small fortune in hundred-dollar bills. You've no idea what can be bought with hundred-dollar American bills in Europe! I'm going to make my whole family comfortable for life, I can tell you. It may be foolish to carry them, but that's all bosh. I'm careful."

"Yes," thought Durant, "you're blessed careful! You don't even talk about it!" Something eluded him here—he could sense it. Larson was right enough about the American money being in keen demand; yet there was some subtly felt note in the whole thing that rang queer.

Durant, cynical enough about most things from his years of bitter struggle with the world, believed in luck. Luck, and no doing of his, had brought him his present affluence. Luck had brought him into contact with Helen Glincka; luck had shown him her story, had given him the chance to serve her. And now, as the boat-train roared on Londonward, luck suddenly bobbed up with the most amazing twist of all.

"Another three-quarters of an hour," said Larson, glancing at his watch. "Hm! Fifteen years since I've been in England, and it looks the same—the same—"

The man's face changed suddenly. His words died. He jerked his hat a little lower, then turned, staring from the window. Durant blinked at him, wondering at his manner, wondering at the odd something about the man. Then he glanced up.

Outside their compartment door was standing a man, looking in. An ordinary Englishman, clipped gray mustache, lounge-suit, square chin, heavy-lidded eyes—only the eyes were not ordinary, for they were the eyes of one who gives orders. A retired army man, perhaps.

He pushed open the door, and came in. His gaze swept Durant, seemed to comprehend him at once, went on to Larson. Durant moved over to make room—the man had come in to smoke, no doubt, as this was a smoker, and the train was fairly full. Next instant, however, Durant realized his mistake. Upon the little compartment settled an atmosphere tense and terrible.

Sitting opposite Larson, the Englishman produced a cigarette and lighted it, indeed—but his eyes were fastened upon Larson, with a grimly humorous expression. Larson gazed at him blankly an instant, then looked away, yet with an effort.

"A bit older, old chap, aren't you?" said the Englishman suddenly. "I fancy we both are, what? Fifteen years—devilish long time, eh?"

Coming so soon after Larson's remark, these words startled Durant, showed him something lay under the surface here. And in the eyes of Larson, he saw it was tragedy.

"I'm afraid you're mistaken," said Larson.

The Englishman laughed, and at the sound of it, Durant stiffened.

"Really, now? Quite a stroke of luck, this—looking for some one else, you know. So your memory has gone off a bit, eh? Most extra'nary, memory! Now, the moment I saw you, I told myself there was my old friend Gunnar Hanson. And what may you be doing in Blighty, Gunnar? Hadn't you fancied it might be a bit unhealthy here, eh?"

"I—I'm going through," said Larson in a strangled voice. "To the Continent. I've made my pile in the States—I'm going through. Not stopping at all."

"Ah, but you're mistaken about that!" said the other pleasantly. "Badly mistaken, old thing! A little matter—what was the name? Inspector Bagwell, wasn't it? I remember his funeral quite well. I promised his widow that I'd bag you some day!" Smiling cheerfully at his victim, the Englishman put his cigarette between his lips and puffed at it—unfortunately for himself. For Larson, though white as a sheet, lashed out a blow as swift and unexpected as the stroke of a snake.

Larson lashed out a blow as swift and unexpected as the stroke of a snake

One short, swift blow—no more. To it, the Englishman crumpled up and sagged limply to one side. Larson's fist showed the gleam of knuckles, as he darted up and to the door. He drew the blue curtains, then whirled, and stared at Durant with a face of desperation.

Durant was laughing—the mad humor of it struck him in a wave. Here was a murderer, a criminal with a record; and Makoff had picked on him as an innocent victim!

"Well, what about it?" snarled the voice of Larson. The latter was suddenly transformed—the shrewd, gentle, unsophisticated old man had become a crouching, desperate enemy of society. "What you going to do, huh? My only chance was to stop his mouth. You heard him—it was fifteen years ago! They'd nab me for that. You're a lord—you can save me or not. What about it?"

Durant's mirth was abruptly banished, and he stared at Larson. The man actually believed Makoff's story, then.

"I'm no policeman," he said. "I suppose you've been a virtuous angel the past fifteen years, eh? Really a manufacturer?"

"Hell, no!" snapped Larson, wide-eyed. "You mean it—you'll give me a chance? I ain't lying. I'm a crook—but you invited me. You liked me. Now, will you stick to it or not?"

Shrewd, this! Thinking Durant an Englishman, a mistake no Briton would have made, and really a lord,—a mistake only an American could have made,—Larson was appealing to his pride, his sporting instinct of fair play and word given.

"What the devil are you?" demanded Durant. "A Dane, as you posed?"

"Yes, by birth. I'm a naturalized American now. Yes or no?"

"Yes," said Durant, "—provided you don't murder this chap."

"Done with you," said Larson.

He darted to the prostrate man, frisked him quickly and efficiently, snapped the steel bracelets around their owner's wrists, emptied the pockets into his own, gagged him with handkerchiefs, stretched him out along one seat after throwing up the arms. To Durant it was a revelation—it showed the man as nothing else could have done. Crook, eh? Then Larson was no petty scoundrel. He knew how to do things.

He snapped the steel bracelets around the owner's wrists and gagged him with handkerchiefs.

Once more the humor of it smote Durant hard, with added force after Larson's statement. The man was a professional crook, self-admitted, and Makoff had selected him—but wait! Crook or not, he had swallowed the bait and was hooked, thus to an extent justifying Makoff's judgment. And Durant himself had been completely deceived by the rascal.

"Just what sort of crook are you?" asked Durant, extending his cigarette-case. He gave no heed to the senseless detective—Durant had little pity for inefficiency. "Bank-robber, confidence-worker or thug?"

Larson grinned, as he flung his overcoat over the unfortunate Englishman and settled down in comfort.

"To tell you the truth, a little of anything," he said frankly. His shrewd old features settled back into their usual kindly wrinkles. "I've touched all sides of the game—but while I'm with you, I'm straight. That goes! I shouldn't have stopped off in England at all, but I thought it was safe enough—and I was tempted. Now, if you and I go together, say by air, we'll get out of the country. That is, if you'll help me so far! Otherwise, I'm done for. It'll be almost impossible for me to get out of England now, unless—"

He made a gesture toward the shape beside him. Durant shook his head.

"None of that. I'll get you out, all right. So you've made your pile in the States, eh? In what game?"

"All kinds," said Larson, and laughed. Then he sobered. "Look here! We'll have to make a quick get-away when we get to the station—Waterloo, is it? Or Paddington? Porters will come through to get luggage and see if anything's left in the cars."

"Don't worry," said Durant calmly. "My chauffeur should meet us there. And to you, I'll be plain Ralph Durant, understand? What's more, I'll keep your secret. Is it agreed?"

"Agreed," said Larson, and put out his hand. "I'll be on the level with you." Durant meant his words. He had no intention whatever of telling Makoff anything, and he shook hands gravely with the murderer and criminal opposite. As a matter of fact, he much preferred the man to Makoff.

Durant had hitherto seen Makoff as a man of culture, energy, ruthless ability; but in the ensuing hours he began to realize why this man could hold his cousin's widow in bonds of blackmail and force her to give not only money, but service, to his cause.

He knew Makoff could have had less than twenty-four hours to prepare for his *coup* against Larson. He knew, too, that Makoff was scrupulously anxious to keep any breath of police suspicion from his activities; much of his work lay among the upper strata of society, and he could not afford publicity or suspicion. Therefore, even granted that he was in touch with some criminal organization in London, his achievement was marvelous.

Having only hand-baggage, Larson and Durant slipped out of the train and down the platform in all haste; they would have only a few moments before the plight of the unfortunate detective was discovered, and swiftness was imperative. Before they had gone the length of the train, however, a neatly liveried chauffeur appeared and saluted Durant as though from old acquaintance.

"All ready, Your Lordship."

"Ah, Giles, how are you?" exclaimed Durant. Inspecting the man, he found him to be no Englishman, certainly—a Continental of some sort. "Here, Larson, turn over your bags to Giles. Is the house opened up for me, Giles?"

"Quite, sir. And the other guests, sir? You cabled one or two others might arrive—"

"Haven't heard yet, Giles," said Durant, and could have laughed to see the expression on Larson's face—half admiring, half delighted. "Lord Tiverton hasn't shown up?"

"No sir, but I have a letter—it came this morning, and as it seemed rather important, I took the liberty to bring it along, sir."

"Give it to me at the car. Hurry, now! Let's get out of this crowd."

Durant let Giles lead the way, and followed with Larson. He did not half like the looks of this tall, rangy chauffeur with a cast in one eye—the man looked altogether too intelligent to be a petty scoundrel. Durant sized him up as a Bulgar or Austrian, from his perfect English and the general cut of his jib.

In another two minutes they were out of the station and climbing into a waiting Daimler saloon that had all the appearance of a luxurious private car. When he had stowed the bags, Giles handed in a letter, closed the door, mounted to his seat, and they moved off. Durant found the letter a registered envelope addressed to Lord Northcote, at an address in King's Road, Richmond.

"Excuse me, will you?" he said, and tore it open in some wonder. He found a page enclosed bearing the following typed message, unaddressed and unsigned:

> Glincka comes tomorrow guest. Also Count Dardent. House small. Others may come. Giles full charge everything.

As Durant pocketed the letter, it occurred to him that Makoff must have chalked up a pretty telegraph bill from Plymouth.

"Lord, how it's changed in fifteen years!" exclaimed Larson, staring out at the streets. Thin rain was falling. "The busses—would you look at 'em! Block the streets, almost—bigger than the houses! Where are we heading?"

"Richmond," said Durant. "I've a small place there. By the way, I think Baroness Glincka will show up tomorrow, for the week-end, and perhaps Count Dardent. One or two others—hard to say. My return seems to have been advertised. You know Richmond?"

"No, but I used to know a man there." Larson fingered his white mustache, and flung Durant a smile. "Chap named Silver—a Scotchman who managed opera tours and such. I trimmed him at a game once. Well, I expect he's dead long ago! Damnable luck running into that chap on the train—used to be a Scotland Yard man. Wonder what he is now? A baronet, maybe."

"You don't seem worried," said Durant.

The other shrugged.

"Not a bit. I've got two passports—different names, different faces. Inside half an hour every passport bureau in the country will be looking out for my face and Larson's name; I couldn't get out of England on that passport if I wanted to! But on the other, and with you to help, it'll work. Anything will work with one of the nobility in it."

"As court records prove!" And Durant chuckled. "Right-ho! We'll see."

The big Daimler purred along; Kensington Park fell behind; on to Hammersmith, on out past new built-up additions until the white square tower of Richmond church hove into sight past a long bend of highway. Durant knew barely enough of London to follow the road with understanding, and Larson did not cease to exclaim over the changes of fifteen years.

"Look here!" Larson turned suddenly. "You have a safe in your place, I suppose?"

Durant assented, trusting to luck.

"Well, I'd like you to take charge of my wad while I'm here," went on the other. "I have a bit over sixty thousand, and—"

"Jumping Jerusalem!" ejaculated Durant, in stark amazement. "Sixty thousand dollars?" "In hundred-dollar bills, mostly—for spending on the Continent," said Larson.

"I want to take care of my family there, buy 'em land, spend all I want, and so forth."

"Good Lord, man, you must have cracked a bank!"

Larson chuckled. "No, not exactly. There's been big money in liquor, you know. I made that sixty thousand, and a bit over, in three months, just to show! Well, if you'll stow the coin away, I'll feel better—I know these English servants, and I'd hate to trust 'em. While I can keep it under my eye, all right, but traveling here ain't safe."

Durant nodded. This request complicated the situation a bit. Beyond keeping Larson from being murdered, he had previously had little interest in the matter. Finding the man's actual status, he had been cynically delighted at the game in prospect, since Makoff was likely to catch a Tartar. Now it seemed as though Larson would succeed in robbing himself—if Durant let the Russian know about the request.

He decided instantly to do no such thing. The outcome of the whole scheme was immaterial to him, though his sympathy was rather with Larson. Besides—why could not Larson be the man to put a bullet into Makoff? Possibilities here, but he would have to see Helen first. If Makoff were dead, the blackmail might only be transferred.

He threw over the whole problem as the car turned sharply out of the highway, between a pub and a brick wall, heading up the long hill of King's Road, lined on either side with its walled English houses and gardens, dismal from the outside, comfortable and rich within, each one having that sense of privacy and ownership which means so little to the American, so much to his

English cousin. Abruptly the car halted before a low house of gray brick, walled about, and Giles held open the door.

"Welcome home, Your Lordship!" he said cheerfully.

The two men left the car, entered the gate, walked up to the house. The door was opened by a maid, who curtsied; Durant saw at a glance that she was French, and nodded to her. Giles brought up their bags.

How Makoff had managed this at so short notice was a marvel to Durant. The house seemed unpretentious but comfortable, and was excellently furnished; the living-room windows gave glimpses of a well-kept garden behind, with walks and fountain.

"You've a room ready for Mr. Larson?" said Durant to the maid. "Good."

She led them upstairs to two adjoining bedrooms; Giles put Larson's grips in one, those of Durant in the other. Then he disappeared. The maid spoke to Durant: "We've kept luncheon waiting, sir."

"Right," said Durant heartily. "We'll have a wash and be right down. Make yourself at home here, Larson—no ceremony. Come down when you're ready."

"Thanks."

Larson's door closed. Durant turned to the maid, who had waited, and spoke in French:

"Will M. Makoff be here?"

"Tomorrow, m'sieur," she responded. "But he will not be seen."

He nodded, and she departed. So she was in the outfit too!

In fifteen minutes Durant and his guest were sitting in a long, low dining-room that overlooked the garden, while the belated luncheon was served. Larson was full of admiration over the place, as well he might be; his first awe had departed, and he threw off restraint. Under his taciturn exterior he revealed a shrewd personality, as thoroughly American as that of Durant himself. He had spent fifteen years in America, ten years previous to that in England, while his education at home in Denmark had been excellent. To realize that he sat opposite a murderer, criminal, bootlegger, a charming old man who had made an excellent unmoral living off society, was continually astonishing to Durant. And Larson had asked no questions about his host or the reason for an incognito—if he was curious, he bottled it up. So Durant conjured up a history for himself, and it was accepted without a word.

"You know, I liked you at the start!" said Larson, when they lighted cigars and adjourned to the garden for a look around. "You know Makoff well?"

"Not well," said Durant. "I met him aboard the boat. Why?"

"I don't cotton to him," said the other. "He may be a nobleman and all that, and the cousin of Baroness Glincka—that the name?—but I know a crook when I see one. I'd ought to, eh? Yes sir. That bird, for all his society airs, is a bad one."

"I believe you," said Durant with a chuckle. Wary Makoff! The Russian had sensed this suspicion in Larson, and did not intend to show himself as a guest. "Makoff wont show up here, I'm glad to say. How do you know I'm not a crook too?"

Larson glanced at him and grinned. "You've the makings of one, and a good one—but I know a square-shooter when I see him! Let's go attend to that money, shall we?"

Durant nodded, and they went upstairs. He brought one of his own bags into Larson's room—a bag specially made, with Yale lock, though Durant had nothing in it except clothes. Being fully aware, by sharp experience, of the fallacious tourist belief that English-made clothes were better than American, he had loaded up at home with a large outfit.

Larson opened a suitcase and threw out on the bed half a dozen packages wrapped in oiled silk and sealed. He broke one open to reveal crisp new hundred-dollar bills.

"Six of 'em," he said. "Open the others up if you like. Why the suitcase?"

"To hold them until I can get into the safe," said Durant. "Better so."

"Suit yourself."

"What sort of receipt do you want?"

"Receipt, hell!" ejaculated Larson. "Don't be a fool. I don't need any receipt from you."

Durant calmly opened all the packages, found them to be as stated, and then stowed them away in his grip, which he replaced in his room, after locking. He chuckled again to think what Makoff would say to this simple acquisition—after so much pains and expense had been bestowed to get Larson in a murder-trap!

"Decidedly," he said cynically, "it pays to be an honest man!"

Had Larson been anything but what he was, the composition of Lord Northcote's week-end party must have struck him as very singular, to say the least.

The only woman in the party was Baroness Glincka, who arrived for luncheon on Saturday. Count Dardent proved to be a worn-out, waspish little man with waxed mustaches and dyed hair, who spoke fair English and fluent Danish; he was French, and Durant made a shrewd guess that he had left Paris very much for his health's sake, not to mention his liberty. He noted that Helen Glincka very obviously disliked the little count.

After their day together, Larson and Durant had become almost intimate.

Durant, at least, found his liking for the shrewd old rascal increased by acquaintance. Nothing had appeared in the newspapers in regard to the finding of a trussed-up detective aboard the boat-train, but this meant nothing, except that an extensive secret search was being made for Gunnar Hanson. No further word had come to Durant via Giles or the maid. No other guests arrived, and the four sat down to dinner Saturday night with Durant very much in the dark as to plans. Larson, however, was clearly charmed by thus mixing with Continental and English nobility, and enjoyed himself hugely.

Dinner was nearly over, when Giles leaned above Durant's chair.

"There's a gentleman asking for you, sir. In the library."

Durant rose, excused himself without the fact appearing strange, and passed into the library. He found Makoff awaiting him.

"Ah!" exclaimed the Russian. "Glad to find everything smooth. No trouble?"

"None, with your perfect arrangements."

"I'll have to turn over the job to you and Michael after all," said Makoff. "I've been called to Paris in haste—making the nine o'clock Southampton train tonight."

"Who's Michael?"

"Giles," and Makoff chuckled. "Good man, eh? Dardent's our regular London agent. Michael has full instructions; I'll give you yours now. Larson, I believe, has fifteen or twenty thousand dollars in currency—"

"Sixty," said Durant. Makoff whistled.

"Sixty thousand? Whew! Still better." He winked delightedly, rubbed his hands. "This house was taken in his name, understand? The cook and so forth engaged in his name. Now—what's the matter?"

"Nothing," said Durant, repressing his consternation at this news. "I was wondering what he'd say if he knew!"

Makoff chuckled. "The cook will be discharged tomorrow night. The maid goes with Dardent—she's his wife, by the way. The Baronne leaves tomorrow night also, via Southampton, for Paris. You and Michael will be here Monday morning. When Larson drinks his early tea, he's done for. Places are already booked for you and Michael on the noon plane from Croydon for Paris. It'll be another day or two at least before Larson's body is discovered, perhaps much longer. You and Michael will bring the stuff. Your seat in the plane is booked in your own name, Michael's in that of Giles Hopper—his passport identity. All clear?"

"Quite," said Durant, "except the necessity for murder. Why not rob him and go? Murder in England means that the law will be at your heels for life."

"Certainly." Makoff eyed him with a grim smile. "But why talk of murder, my dear man? An empty vial of chloral, purchased in a New York drug-store; a dead American, who has rented a house for three months and occupied it for three days; a letter stating that speculations in exchange have wiped out his fortune—who would call it murder? Guests, servants, all dissipated as a dream!"

"It is artistic, certainly." Durant's tone was dry. "I only objected to so much work. Why bother to kill him?"

"Because Americans have loud voices." Makoff chuckled. "And certainly we do not want the law after us! Surely you can realize this?"

Durant nodded and banished his frown. "Right! Indeed, it is magnificent. This Michael is an admirable fellow—I congratulate you on having him. He handles details wonderfully!"

"He should," said Makoff. "He's no other than Michael Korin, who killed Grand Duke Vassily last year in Tours and turned over all his papers to me. Well, I've no time to lose. Give my regards to the charming Baronne—and this envelope. It's her passage to Paris."

Durant took the envelope, shook hands with Makoff and returned to the dinner-table.

Inwardly he was in a ferment of anxiety and excitement; had it been his own neck in peril, he would have lost no whit of his usual icy coolness—but here was another matter. By this time, perhaps, the fact would be known that Larson had rented a house in Richmond—and Scotland Yard would be down on him full force. Had Boris Makoff only known it, he could have robbed Larson with absolute impunity!

Durant looked at Giles, too, with new eyes, appreciating now the frightful danger from this man. He knew of Grand Duke Vassily's murder—all Europe knew of it! The exiled Russian noble had been hideously murdered and robbed—a crime so horribly brutal, so well conceived and executed, that it was supposed to have been perpetrated by Soviet agents. Indeed, the name of Korin had been mentioned as that of the murderer, but the man had never been found.

Things were getting a bit thick, thought Durant to himself. In other words, the simple situation was becoming extremely complex and correspondingly threatening. The only relief in sight was that by Sunday night the group would be scattered, leaving him and Larson alone here with Giles—or Michael Korin. Yet would it be safe for Larson to remain here another twenty-four hours? There was the rub.

The quartet adjourned to the garden for coffee. While Dardent and Larson were deep in floods of Danish, the Baronne was temporarily left to Durant.

"It's confounded hard to get a word with you!" he complained, handing her the envelope. "You're booked for Southampton-Havre tomorrow night."

Her eyes questioned him anxiously. "And you?"

"Paris on Monday. I'll show up, never fear! But Boris has caught a Tartar this time and doesn't know it, so I'm afraid you wont see our honest Giles again."

"Explain!"

"Sha'n't do it. I'm going by results. I intend to show up in Paris and open the fight on Boris—"

"You won't find him!" she breathed. "He disappears. No one knows—"

"Tell that to the marines," said Durant confidently. "Now, you suggest a motor-trip tomorrow—I want to get out of here for the day. Anywhere!"

The others rejoined them, and the coffee finished, they went into the house and settled down to an evening of bridge. Durant had no more chance that evening for a word with her—he had more than a suspicion, indeed, that Giles was keeping a sharp eye on the Baronne. The motor trip was settled upon for the next morning, with general acclaim.

It was late when the game broke up, and Durant saw his supposed guests to their rooms, then turned in, dismissing his problems. He did not waken until roused at seven-thirty by Giles, who bore his "early tea" after the approved English fashion. Then he sat up in bed.

"Shut the door—that's right! Look here, these Americans aren't used to the English custom of early tea, and I'm afraid your scheme will slip up in the morning. Suppose you fix us up some coffee tonight, after we take Baroness Glincka to her train—eh? That would make the matter more certain."

"Good," approved the other, his high cheek-bones lending his aquiline face a distinctly Tartar look. "Yes, a good idea. Thank you!"

Twenty minutes later, after a light knock at the adjoining door, Durant stepped into Larson's room. Larson was shaving, and nodded cheerfully to him. Durant lighted a cigarette, drew up a chair, and played the idea that had come to him.

"What do you think of that man of mine—Giles?"

Larson grimaced. "If you ask me, I think he's a crook!"

"He is." Durant laughed. "I overheard an interesting conversation this morning. It seems that tonight, after our party breaks up, a nice little game is to be played on you and me. Giles will fix us up some coffee and sandwiches, and when we go to bed, we'll stay a long time—long enough for the getaway."

Larson, holding his razor in air, turned and stared at him.

"Is that straight? Would they pull that stuff on a lord?"

"You ought to know—you've lived in England."

"Hm! Good gosh, man—do they know about my money?"

"Probably suspect you have some, while they know I have some," said Durant. "What's more, I gather that our friend Giles is wanted by the police in several countries. Rather interesting to think what might have happened, eh? I'll turn him over to the police—"

"Don't do that!" Larson faced him earnestly. "Not until I'm safe, anyhow. Don't you know their ways here? All hands would be gone over with a fine-tooth comb, and that'd mean my finish!"

"Oh!" said Durant. "But what to do, then?"

"Take him with us," said Larson promptly, and his blue eyes sparkled. "We'll take the Baroness to her train, see? But we'll have our own luggage aboard too. Then you spring it on Giles that we're going somewhere for the night—we can go to a hotel—and tell him to meet us tomorrow and go to Paris with us. That'll knock him off his feet, believe me! I thought that fellow had a bad look to his eye, all along."

"All right; we'll drop him in Paris, then. Meantime, about your money: Giles will drive us today, and that's why the place is safe enough until tonight. We'll go over by air, and there's no Customs examination that way; better make the money into a separate packet and take it with you, however, as the luggage is packed in a separate compartment."

Larson nodded, and his wrinkled, shrewd old face cracked in a grin. "Fine, My Lord, fine! We'll have some fun, eh?" Durant rather thought they would—before it was over.

At ten that Sunday morning the big Daimler, with the lunch packed and aboard, was standing before the gate of the King's Road house, and Giles had just announced that all was ready, when Larson flung open the door of Durant's room with an excited word.

"Durant! Come here—quick!"

Durant joined him. Standing well back from a window, which overlooked the street, Larson pointed. No words were needed. Coming up the hill, and looking at the house with evident interest, was the man they had left trussed and gagged aboard the boat-train.

"Pinched!" said Larson.

"Not yet." Durant turned. "Shut your door—get packed!"

He darted to the stairs. "Giles! Here—quick, man!"

Michael Korin came up on the jump, and Durant pulled him into his bedroom.

"Look at that man across the street. Know him?"

One look, and the Russian drew back, a gray pallor in his face.

"Sacred name of a dog!" he exclaimed. "Yes! That's Sir John Brentwood himself—of Scotland Yard."

Durant gripped him by the arm, hard. "All right. Brace up, now! He's looking the place over—we have time to get away. Something's slipped; perhaps they're after you, perhaps after me. We'll get our luggage aboard the car, drop Baronne Glincka downtown, drop Dardent and his wife, get out to Croydon and make the noon plane. Understand? I'll telephone for bookings. Warn Dardent, get rid of the cook instantly, clear the place. Go!"

The man slipped away, obviously badly shaken by what he had seen. Durant turned into Larson's room.

"Get ready! I've got your money in my bag. We're off in five minutes."

"I'll need ten," said Larson, calmly enough. "I must get rid of this mustache, clap on some hair-dye, fix my face."

"Take seven—move like hell!" snapped Durant.

Larson was already plunging for his bag. Catching up his own grips without bothering to pack his scattered belongings, Durant hurried downstairs to the telephone. In two minutes he had the Croydon aërodrome on the line.

"Mr. Durant speaking," he said. "I have bookings for myself and a friend on the noon Paris bus tomorrow. We want to change and go over today. A third may go with us."

"Very sorry, sir, we've just booked the last seat," came the reply. "Hold on just a moment, will you?"

Durant held on, cursing softly to himself. Giles appeared, breathing hard.

"Off in five minutes," he said. Durant nodded. Then came the voice on the wire: "Hello! I think we can take care of you, sir. We're sending over a D H special to bring back a party of officials, and we can put you and the mail-sacks aboard, if you like. Would there be any trunks?"

"No, nothing but hand-luggage," said Durant in sharp relief.

"Can do, sir. She'll take off a bit ahead of the regular bus, though—about eleven-thirty. Can you get out here by eleven?"

"We've our own car," said Durant. "Yes, we can get out by eleven or shortly after."

"Right-ho!"

Durant hung up and glanced at the man beside him.

"Special plane going over to Paris. We must get to Croydon at eleven. You, I, Larson."

"Good," said the Russian. "I'll arrange to have the Daimler picked up at the aërodrome—it's a rented car. Or Dardent can attend to that detail."

"We'd better all go out at once, carry our luggage, pile in and be off," said Durant. "The house is being watched—you'll have to make a dash for it and throw 'em off."

Dardent appeared, waspishly excited, and the maid—in reality his wife—followed. Helen Glincka was on the stairs, and Durant took her bags and set them with his own.

"It'll be touch and go," he said, perceiving that the general feeling was that the police were after them all. Naturally, he alone knew the actual facts. "Depends on getting off on the jump. Not a word of anything wrong, now, before Larson! Helen, we'll drop you at the Savoy. Go on to Paris tonight via Havre, as arranged; you're in no danger. Dardent, where'll we drop you?"

"Brompton Road," said the little Frenchman. "Our apartment is there—Michael knows."

"Good. Here's Larson. All together, now—out to the car, pile in anyhow!"

And how Michael drove, out through Victoria and on to Croydon! Durant marveled at it; no American, accustomed to wide highways and a gradual sweep around other cars, could have tooled a car at any speed along these narrow English lanes, except with long practice. With a head-on collision apparently imminent, each car would give a jerky twist, out and back—and they would be past. There was a peculiar knack to it, and the Russian had this knack at his fingers' ends.

"Why the general rush?" inquired Larson, when the two of them were alone in the car. "Everybody seemed in a devil of a hurry to get gone!"

Durant had already prepared for this, and broke into a laugh.

"We had to get out quickly—so I told 'em the cook had developed smallpox. Cleared out the maid and all, as you saw! Our pleasant chauffeur goes over with us. Here's my bag—I'll get out your money. Wrap it in this newspaper."

They suited action to word, Durant having put his own bags inside the car. With a newspaper-wrapped bundle of sixty thousand dollars in his lap, Larson relaxed and lighted a cigarette. Now, for the first time, Durant had a good view of him, and whistled.

"You certainly have changed yourself! Hope you have your extra passport handy."

"No danger. As to the change—that's a cinch."

It was also a complete success, to which Larson now added a pair of black-rimmed spectacles. With his mustache gone and his hair changed from gray to a glossy black, he looked twenty years younger; eyebrows had become black too, and subtle changes in the outline of his face, due probably to wads of cotton against his teeth, gave him an entirely new look, as did the goggles—stamping him in London as an American tourist.

Now they had turned past the Croydon Arms, and the big car thrummed along wide open until the huge gray hangars loomed ahead. They swung in between the rows of low buildings and came to rest in the parking-space beside the office. Two planes were already warming up—a huge silver giant, triple-engined, and a smaller De Haviland, on the concrete take-off. An orange-brown French machine was just circling to land.

"Mr. Durant?" A crisp, energetic youngster pulled open the car door. "Come along and I'll rush you through—plane's waiting now. We'll have you off the ground before the bus gets here for the regular flight. Into the office, please."

"The car will be sent for," said Durant, and the other nodded.

There was no time lost in weighing in and checking the luggage, which was sent on to the Customs shed and put through perfunctorily, as it would be put through at the other end. In three minutes they were crossing to the passport control office. The Russian went through first; and as they waited, Larson jogged Durant's elbow, indicating a man who sat beside the passport officer.

"Scotland Yard," he said under his breath. "Now watch him!"

He followed the Russian, laid down his passport, waited. Though it must have been a tense moment for him, with his neck in the balance, Larson appeared quite cool. The Scotland Yard man glanced at the passport, glanced up at him, then leaned back and gazed out across the flying field, without interest. Stamped and returned, Larson picked up his passport and went on. Durant followed, and was put through without comment.

The three men stepped through the little door, and found their guide awaiting them. But as they followed out to where the machines were idling, the Russian fell back and joined Durant, in savage bewilderment.

"What's it mean?" he snapped in French. "That one?" And he jerked his thumb toward Larson. Then Durant recollected that he must have seen the other's altered appearance for the first time.

"Getting ready for Paris, I suppose," he said with a laugh.

"Ar-r-rgh!" growled Michael Korin. "Think I'm a fool?"

The man strode on, but in his powerful features was stormy mingling of anger, suspicion, fear. Durant shrugged—what matter, now? He had already determined on his course, rightly estimating the Russian as one of Makoff's chief aides, who must be put out of the way now or later. It might better be now. Only the fact of Larson's predicament, indeed, had prevented Durant from putting the London police on the trail of Michael Korin.

When they reached the De Haviland, the pilot was already in place, testing his engine—a youngish man with twinkling blue eyes and a stubby yellow mustache. Their guide turned.

"All's loaded," he shouted. "You'll be off at once."

This eight-passenger car was much smaller than the big machines. All but three of the seats were piled high with luggage and freight, for the balance of the loads was most carefully arranged. Durant was given the empty seat forward, Larson the one just behind, and Michael Korin in the rear. Larson shoved his newspaper-wrapped package in the rack, got rid of his mufflings, and gave the staring Russian a sardonic grin.

That grin, Durant reflected afterward, must have done the business—for Korin was no fool.

The roar of the engines rose to a crescendo, and abruptly the De Haviland moved—glided over the ground, bumped, turned, swept madly across the field, bumped again, took the air. A turn, and with the slight bank Larson gripped his chair-arms hard, then laughed as he met the eyes of Durant.

"New experience for me!" he shouted. Michael Korin sat slumped in his chair, frowning savagely, eyes ablaze with sullen fires as he watched the other two men. The altimeter crept around—one—two—three thousand feet. The pilot unreeled his wireless antennae.

England lay below them.

The De Haviland had the wind with her and was doing her even hundred, so that in less than an hour the yellow sand-beaches of the French coast showed ahead. The glass window of the cockpit showed them the pilot's head, and a notice beside it advised that it be opened for communication if necessary.

Durant took an old envelope from his pocket, and pencil, and began to write. His message was curt and to the point:

> Passenger Hopper is Michael Korin, who murdered Grand Duke Vassily last year. Wanted by all police. Radio Paris police at once to arrest him on arrival.

This done, Durant rose and went forward. He reached up and tried to open the little embrasure, but to no effect. The pilot turned, shrugged, and shook his head, shouting something that was lost.

Unable to pass the envelope through, Durant held it up to the glass. The pilot read it, and his eyes widened. Then he nodded comprehension and turned around again; craning up, Durant watched him lean forward, speaking into the microphone set before him. Already the Channel was far behind, the brown-green field-patches of France flitting past underneath....

To Durant it seemed to happen all in a flash, for he had been intent on what he was doing, and the roaring of the motor drowned out all lesser sounds. There was a rush of movement, the envelope was torn from his hand; losing balance, he staggered for an instant.

Recovering, he saw Michael Korin standing just behind him, glancing at the writing with inflamed eyes—Durant clutched at it, gained it before the Russian had read it—or half of it, at least. In doing so, he lost balance again, to the drop of the plane in an air-pocket, and went sprawling across the freight. As he went down, he saw the figure of Larson, limply sprawled in his seat, head sagging—dead or senseless.

Korin read what was gripped in his hand. It was the top part of the envelope, bearing the first sentence only—but this was quite enough. A scream rang through the cabin, above the thrumming roar of the engine—a scream of wild rage, inarticulate, bestial.

"Traitor!" shouted out the Russian, as Durant got to his feet. "Vile dog of a traitor! What sort of trap have you laid? You want to have me pinched and get away with the money yourself? Or—"

Words, evasion, all useless here! The man was swept by a passion of insane rage; nostrils dilated, lips drawn back in a snarl, eyes aflame, he was out of himself. For an instant Durant, who was unarmed, shrank before the memory of how Grand Duke Vassily had died, his throat torn out by teeth as by the teeth of a wild beast. And here was the wild beast!

Then, braced, Durant leaped and drove in a terrific blow to the stomach. The blow failed. Korin swerved, snapped hand to pocket, jerked out an automatic pistol. Durant's fist smashed on his wrist, and the pistol fell. Then the two men were reeling, grappling, striking, locked in a mad embrace, hurling themselves about the narrow cabin in frenzied desperation of fight, while the earth rolled three thousand feet below.

The two men were reeling, grappling, striking, locked in a mad embrace.

Durant speedily knew that, save for luck, he was mastered. No man could cope with the insane fury of this wild beast—for such Korin had become. Though Durant's fist hammered him relentlessly, sending crushing blows to face and stomach, though he himself knew nothing of fighting, Korin seemed made of living steel. Twice Durant got in smashes to the angle of the jaw, with absolutely no effect. Korin flung him about as though he were a child, swept him off his feet with the sheer force of a wild, flailing swing, picked him up and hurled him against the cockpit wall.

Then, leaping on him, Korin got him about the throat in a fearful throttling grapple, and reached for a grip with his teeth. Frantic, Durant broke the hold with the familiar *jiu-jitsu* break of arms inside arms, brought up his knee in a deadly blow; for an instant thought the fight won. Korin staggered, and Durant deliberately smashed him under the chin and knocked him against one window, smashing the glass; then, even before Durant could follow it up, Korin was back on the rebound in another grapple, with a wild and shrill scream.

Durant glimpsed the face of the pilot staring back through the small glass inset, but the pilot was probably unarmed and helpless to intervene. Helpless, too, to keep the De Haviland on an even keel, for with the wild rushes and swift movements of the two men, she was lurching badly. The newspaper bundle was swept from the rack, and packages of bank-notes lay around.

Curtains were torn down, windows smashed; the body of Larson sprawled on the floor and tripped them as they fought. Then, once more, Korin hurled himself in and grappled, bearing Durant backward off balance. The plane lurched wildly. Both men went headlong, locked together— And Durant, underneath, was pitched head-first into the wall. This ended the fight for him.

When he woke up, realizing that he was not dead, Durant found that he lay half doubled into a seat, wrists and ankles lashed with curtain cords. If he had achieved nothing else, his blows had certainly knocked sanity into the Russian, who was terrifically battered. Some little time must have passed, for as Durant looked, he saw Korin smashing the little glass window of the cockpit, striking at it with his pistol.

"Land!" His voice rose shrill above the engine-roar, as he shoved his weapon into the face of the pilot. "Land at once!"

The air-man shouted a response which Durant could not catch. Korin was altogether too sane not to know that his life depended on that of the pilot— he dared not shoot the little Englishman who defied him.

He cursed, raved, threatened; then, with a wild laugh, he thrust out the pistol and fired, twice.

As the plane lurched, Durant caught his breath, thinking Korin had shot the pilot. But the crafty Russian had done better—he had smashed the propeller.

The wild roar of the engine was succeeded by a swift and terrible silence, through which drove the voice of Michael Korin in a wild blast. There was something splendid and magnificent about the man in this instant, as he stood watching the pilot and laughed in exultation, awaiting the result of his mad challenge to destiny.

"Now land, you swine-dog! Land, and if you try any tricks, you'll get a bullet!"

"Blast you!" came the pilot's voice, but that was all. The air-man was busy.

Korin was beyond thought of anything now except the money scattered about his feet, and what would happen somewhere in France, three thousand feet below. He stooped, caught up the packets of notes, stuffed his pockets with them, then straightened again.

Durant realized now that, given any half-decent landing-place, they stood in little actual danger. It all depended on the landing place—but this was a big gamble. Sharply banked, the De Haviland plunged earthward, gathering speed for the final straightening out; struts and braces quivered, thrummed madly; wind whistled and shrieked through the smashed side windows. His eyes going to the altimeter on the cockpit wall, Durant saw the needle shake and turn, twenty-five hundred—two thousand—fifteen hundred—a thousand feet! The whole ship was roaring, shivering, shrieking to the wild plunge earthward.

Something stirred in Durant's brain—wonder at it. Why would Korin do such an insane thing? He must know that he could not escape, that mere landing would not save him, that at each moment the pilot must have been reporting into the microphone what was going on, that on the earth below must be a scurry of cars and motorcycles, police converging on wherever the landing-place would be! Yet there the Russian stood, furiously exultant, carried out of himself by the sheer sweeping excitement of the moment, pouring forth a stream of laughing oaths as he held himself braced and looked out upon the rising earth!

Then the explanation swept upon Durant in all its simple truth. Korin, as a matter of fact, knew nothing about the microphone! Very few people did know that these planes were so equipped, all of them.

The needle was nearly down, now. Korin was waiting, expectant, hawklike. The ship came to an even keel, floated—the pilot was cursing frantically as he worked. Then silence again, a shout from Korin, a heavy bump—and a crash. No—safe! The ship was bumping, rolling over ground, slowing down.

After this, the end was sharp, swift, dramatic enough even to Durant, who could see nothing of what passed outside the ship. Korin seized a suitcase and beat out the glass of the broken window beside him—needlessly, for he might have drawn the sash—and then crawled out. The voice of the pilot sounded:

"Here, I say! You can't do it, you know—"

Korin laughed, and the sound of a shot brought silence.

A little after, Durant was aware of Larson bending over him, fumbling at his wrists, shaking, excited, yet also laughing.

"Men coming," said Larson. "Two airplanes landing, too—looks like a landing-ground. For the love of heaven, Durant, keep your mouth shut about the money!"

"But he got away with it!" exclaimed Durant. Freed, he sat up, saw the high radio towers and the huts below. "This is Abbeville, just outside town—they can get him. I had the pilot radio his name and—"

"Lay off!" cried Larson frantically. "I got to get to Paris and drop out of sight quick—beat it! Understand? Our pilot ain't dead—he only got a bullet through his leg. Let 'em all think the fellow was just trying to make his getaway—"

"And let the money go?" demanded Durant, incredulous.

"Sure, let it go!" said Larson, with a wink. "I got more of it. Let it go!" Durant shrugged.

Next morning, in his little hotel in the Rue Vignon, behind the Madeleine, Durant caught at the *Echo de Paris* brought with his coffee and rolls. On the front page was the story he sought:

> Michael Korin, the assassin of Grand Duke Vassily, was killed yesterday near Abbeville by *gardes champêtres*, in a running battle.
>
> It was no ordinary, sordid slaying; it was drama! This great criminal was crossing audaciously from London to Paris by avion.
>
> Recognized by one of the passengers, he brought the avion to earth by shooting away the propeller. The pilot, who was wounded, sent the alarm by radio. Unhappily for himself, Korin touched earth at the Abbeville aërodrome.

Durant, thrilled, laid down his paper. Korin was dead, then! And since the names of all air passengers were carefully registered, and the names of all hotel arrivals in Paris were at once deposited with the police, he would soon be traced here and interviewed.

What of Larson, then? Durant chuckled—for Larson was gone. He had slipped out of the Airways bus as it passed the Gare du Nord, after one hasty grip of farewell, and Durant had last seen him darting into the big station. Larson was gone, somewhere, like a rat hunting its hole. Why? He was safe enough here, surely. And he had still some money left. But what about the money Korin had taken? Surely Larson would claim it.

His eye fell on the paper again, and followed down to the final paragraph of the story. He read it, with stupefied astonishment. The whole thing swept upon him then, with stunning force. Here he had the explanation of Larson's puzzling conduct—and the most astounding joke on Boris Makoff! For Makoff, at this very moment, must be reading this news-story too; he would not understand Larson's share in it, perhaps, but he would quite understand for what he had expended money and brains prodigally, not to mention for what Michael Korin had thrown away his life.

"Bootlegging, indeed!" exclaimed Durant, mirth struggling against wonder and admiration. "The clever scoundrel! I bet a dollar he was never fooled a minute about Lord Northcote—I bet he was on to the whole game, and was playing us all for suckers. And this is why he wouldn't claim the money, and why he's probably outside France by this time, passing off his hundred-dollar bills on Belgians or Danes."

For this final paragraph was curtly pointed:

> In the pockets of the dead assassin were found quantities of American bank-notes, amounting to a very large sum. The fact that they were in Korin's possession drew suspicion, and upon examination they have been pronounced forgeries. Undoubtedly Korin had intended passing them off upon our good merchants of Paris.

Durant thought of what Boris Makoff must be saying—and laughed again.

Milton Keynes UK
Ingram Content Group UK Ltd.
UKHW010855010724
444982UK00005B/648